D0392371

Parents and Caregivers,

Stone Arch Readers are designed to provide enjoyable reading experiences, as well as opportunities to develop vocabulary, literacy skills, and comprehension. Here are a few ways to support your beginning reader:

- Talk with your child about the ideas addressed in the story.
- Discuss each illustration, mentioning the characters, where they are, and what they are doing.
- Read with expression, pointing to each word. You may want to read the whole story through and then revisit parts of the story to ensure that the meanings of words or phrases are understood.
- Talk about why the character did what he or she did and what your child would do in that situation.
- Help your child connect with characters and events in the story.

Remember, reading with your child should be fun, not forced. Each moment spent reading with your child is a priceless investment in his or her literacy life.

Gail Saunders-Smith, Ph.D.

written by Melinda Melton Crow
illustrated by Chad Thompson

Production Specialist: Michelle Biedscheid
Designer: Hilary Wacholz
Art Director: Kay Fraser
Laurie K. Holland, Media Specialist
Melinda Melton Crow, M.Ed.
Gail Saunders-Smith, Ph.D.
Reading Consultants:

STONE ARCH READERS

are published by Stone Arch Books
a Capstone imprint
1710 Roe Crest Drive
North Mankato, Minnesota 56003
www.capstonepub.com

Library of Congress Cataloging-in-Publication Data
Crow, Melinda Melton.
Lucky School Bus / by Melinda Melton Crow ; illustrated by Chad Thompson.
p. cm. — (Stone Arch readers. Wonder wheels)
Summary: "School Bus is ready for his big job on the first day of school"—Provided by publisher.
ISBN 978-1-4342-3026-3 (library binding)
ISBN 978-1-4342-3381-3 (pbk.)
[1. First day of school—Fiction. 2. School buses—Fiction. 3. Schools—Fiction.] I. Thompson, Chad, 1974- ill. II. Title.
PZ7.C88536Lu 2011
[E]—dc22   2010050151

Printed in the United States of America in Stevens Point, Wisconsin.
112011   006475R

STONE ARCH BOOKS
a capstone imprint

Lucky School Bus

School Bus, Tractor, Fire Truck, and Train are friends.

Wonder Wheels Garage

It was the first day of school.

School Bus was ready.

"School Bus is lucky,"
said Tractor.

"He has a special job,"
said Train.

"Goodbye!" said School Bus.

"Good luck!" said Fire Truck.

School Bus went to work.

School Bus took the children to school.

After school, he brought
them home safely.

"Here comes School Bus,"
said Fire Truck.

"How was your day?"
said Train.

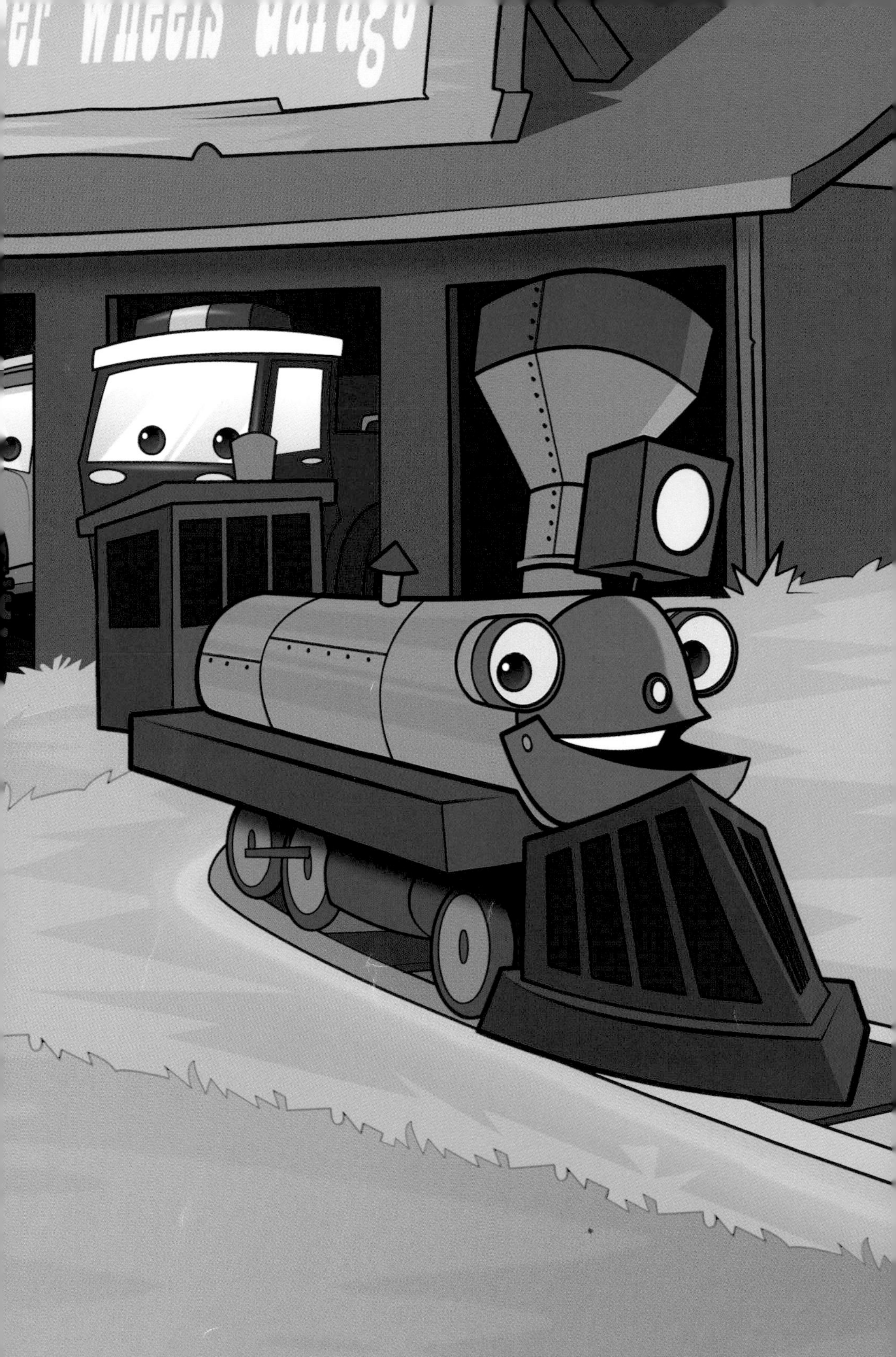
er Wheels Garage

"Great!" said School Bus.

"I can not wait for tomorrow!"
said School Bus.

STORY WORDS

friends   lucky   safely

school   special   tomorrow

Total Word Count: 87